The Train to Nowhere

Gigi Cheng

ISBN: 9781087932996 (Paperback)

Library of Congress Control Number: 2022907195

Published by Gigi Cheng

Dear readers,

This book heavily contains the following topics: suicide, depression, anxiety, PTSD, sexual abuse, violence, death, and gore. Please proceed with caution and understanding that the content is dark and heavy. It will be uncomfortable at times; however, I believe these topics are crucial to discuss and share. This book is about my personal experiences, and my hope is that it could shed some light on what it is like and create more awareness. Please be thoughtful and understanding if you choose to read this book. My advice is to read *slowly* and *carefully*.

Finally, I will be here with you throughout your experience with this book, so don't be afraid. I promise, there's a happy ending.

Spread some love and kindness,

Gigi Cheng

For my family, my friends, my boyfriend, and
Edward, whom I've learned to live with.

Introduction

On February 21, 2021, I decided to commit suicide. It was around 5:20 a.m. in the morning of that Sunday. I took a knife and slit my left wrist. I was fortunate enough to have bandage wraps nearby. By the time the ambulance arrived, I had stopped my own bleeding. They took me to the hospital to get stitches done.

I've had to deal with a lot before that moment. I could barely pay any attention in school with the amount of medication I was on, and all I wanted was to go home to hurt myself. I was absent a lot, too. I couldn't leave my house.

I'm in a better place now. I don't think I'm completely there yet, but maybe, no one ever is and that's okay. I have a wonderful family that has supported me through this whole journey and an amazing boyfriend who's always there for me.

I wrote this book to inspire. I promise, it really does get better.

Contents

In Between Worlds

Abandoned Station

I don't know what it is about sound. It blurs the rest of my senses, like attempting to draw in charcoal for the first time and accidentally smudging thumb-sized marks all over it. I heard her singing, first. I thought it was a guy with how low and almost intoxicating it was. I almost felt tipsy from it, charmed maybe, lured in. I don't think there was any way out of it. Her voice mixed in with the unending, rhythmic sound of a bass, harmonizing with whatever key kept jamming itself into my ears. That was the first layer. There were many more. I heard a father talking to their child—oh yeah. Children, the sound of kids, holding their twenty-dollar souvenir like a trophy, exclaiming with joy of the festivities, though they probably had no idea what the significance of any of it was. The vendors proudly boasting their work, or even the silence of them simply waiting and sitting there was a sound itself. Onlookers, passerby, customers, students, teachers, old, young—whatever you'd like to call them. They talked endlessly. "I love your work! What is the idea behind it?" "There is no way that is so expensive. Why is it so expensive?" "You'd be surprised." "Thank you so much!" They mixed and mingled and separated like the way water does, conjoining, splitting, reforming…

I don't know what is about sound.

Next thing I knew, my vision was inebriated. A trance, maybe. Something like that. Colors popped and faded; figures moved like tall grass under the wind's siege after having been ignored for weeks. I can't explain how it felt. Terrifying, maybe. Something relieving and free as well. All I can say was that I heard my name in the middle of the carnival-like chaos that my mind was envisioning, intertwining, and manipulating into the reality of things. It was quiet, but I could hear it.

"_____."

I suppose I could've ignored it. I could've ignored it in that I didn't have to respond, just as I didn't respond to the many other voices I heard. Not the mother scolding her eight-year-old because he wanted the succulent toolkit that was selling for a hefty twenty. Not the stream of my classmates commenting and laughing among themselves (what are they even talking about?) Just—my name. Of course, I followed it. I'm not the brightest. No matter what angle you looked at me, I was just a kid.

Behind the building, I detached myself from the mass body of mixes. I don't think I was ever attached to them anyways. In my wandering, I found a sight that rooted me against my will.

Train tracks.

That and utility poles. Big, then medium, then small. Electric wires of different sizes weaved frantically between and beyond and across. The street was very narrow. The buildings were an achromatic shade, something muted, something that felt natural, but on the top part, the shade glowed with highlighter yellow. It wasn't brown anymore, or a disgusting garnet. It was bold, popping, and tickled the artist in me. The sound of the street performer was prominent, alongside the others behind me, bumbling around like schools of fish searching for food. Still, all of that was a wall away. I was *in between worlds.*

I stepped over the edge of the track and onto the metal plank that peeked from the mix of weed, leaves, and litter. Then, my other foot. I looked down the tracks, the street, the utility poles. I didn't know where this led, but something was still calling me.

"_____."

It was almost as intoxicating as the girl who sang.

I started walking. Left foot, right foot, one after another onto the plank, and other times, skipping the plank. There were bubble gum wrappers, autumn leaves that were branched out, creating a shape my mind couldn't understand, grass, at least, I thought they were grass, creeping from under and over the sides of the train tracks. They occasionally tickled my ankles, brushing them, giving them a gentle kiss only to disappear from my memory. There were glass shards, remnants of empty beer cans, perhaps a new home for wandering insects. Blackbirds in groups of three waddled the vicinity. Some flew off, many huddled on top of the electric wires, creating a shadow on top of the weed representing a loose line with inconsistent increments of blobs.

After a while, the train tracks split. The left side disappeared into the mound of peach colored dirt and rocks and wildflower. The other led to a station. I took right. It stopped abruptly at the end of the station. It was a beautiful station. There were rusted columns of metalwork that must've held this station up for decades. The concrete had years' worth of graffitI of flowers, peace signs, and inevitably, the male genital. Most noticeably, there was one pressed against the surface of the garage door of the station.

It read: "NOWHERE." I liked it. It looked messy, done in bright candy red. It called me.

I heard a crunch in my next step and looked down to find a newspaper. There was a quarterback pictured on the front. I don't know why I bent down to investigate or read the content, considering I didn't even like football. I still did. On the side, I noticed a small article with the title: "18-YEAR-OLD GIRL FOUND DEAD." I read it out loud.

"At around 5:20 a.m. on February 21, 2021, the police department of ________ rushed to the house of ____ after receiving a desperate call for help. ___ was found dead in her bedroom, having bled out from a deep cut in her left wrist. It was pronounced a suicide. HI ___. I know you're reading this right now. I am excited to meet you. A train will pick you up soon. Please cooperate. Until then. Edward."

I heard a bell chime and stood up instinctively. I finally became aware of my surroundings, of how dangerous it was for me to wander off, of of of—of how my classmates were gone and I was alone. Slowly, the world shifted. I found myself standing in nowhere. The tracks and the utility poles seemed to float on an eternal floor that I stood on, stretching for miles on end. The ground had a liquid-like characteristic and reflected the few buildings and other items that had stayed. The people attending the festivities were gone, the sound of the live performer, the conversations, the tantrums and scolding were gone.

I was alone.

I heard the whistle of a train from a far distance. Within minutes, it materialized from my left. It was headed directly towards me with blistering speed. I climbed on the ladder without thinking and tumbled onto the station just in time for the train to arrive where I was standing only a second ago. It was loud and demanded the absolute attention of all my senses. It was a typical train you'd find on television and shows, jet black with the word "NOWHERE" written in gold across its surface. There were foggy windows, and it looked like there were no passengers. It sighed as it came to halt. The doors swung opened. For a moment, nothing happened. The air stood still and held its breath. Everything waited for my response, but I stood there on my heels, rooted, planted, and afraid. The train whistled again, so loud that I felt the vibrations in my bone, and it kicked me off the ground and into the train. The door closed behind me, and the train began to move. I had no choice but to quickly take the nearest seat. I held my breath and closed my eyes. It was nothing but a dream.

I opened them and found a soft golden ticket in my hands. There were botches of black, grey, and rufous red. It looked like blood. I dropped it instinctively out of surprise, but I bent down to read what it said.

"One-way ticket to the

City of Nowhere."

Nowhere

The Train to Nowhere

I am riding a train to Nowhere,
to Nowhere I will go.
I will sit here till I age,
my bones dried and I'm old.

I am riding a train to Nowhere,
for I have nowhere to be.
I hear a voice calling my name,
but it does not matter to me.

For I am riding a train to Nowhere,
it leaves a trailing sigh.
The window's vivid streaks of blue
then orange into night.

I am riding a train to Nowhere,
with passengers that come and leave.
The monsters, people, old or young
have places they need to be.

I wonder what it means.
Where people go when they leave?
Why some are demons and or ghosts?
What everyone outside sees?

How I wish to see the painting!
Or the mirror underneath!
But this train that takes me Nowhere,
how I'm afraid to ever leave.

I am riding a train to Nowhere,
to Nowhere I will go.
I have stayed here for too long
so long that I've grown mold.

I am riding a train to Nowhere,
to Nowhere is where it ends.
Here at the stop, a city,
a place for me to rest.

City of Nowhere

This is the City of Nowhere
with no one, nothing, and none.
The buildings are a miserable grey
leaning to and forth and from.

The empty streets are flooded.
The people bear no face.
Their nose and eyes and mouths and ears
are scribbled by stains of grey.

A girl beside me was ran over.
The guy ahead shot dead.
A beggar to the left of me,
a severed neck without a head.

In this City of Nowhere,
people hang from the lights.
The weather forecast is often
raining people from the heights.

I found an apartment to stay in
next to a café and corner-store.
I heard the currency here are eyeballs
but ears and fingers are worth more.

The alarm clock wakes me up
to another day dead.
In the closet I find a row of
apathy in bright red.

This City of Nowhere
is nowhere you'd want to go.
But here in this ignorant place,
I have no other home.

Dear ____,

I see you've arrived. I'm very glad. I was beginning to become bored. Course, for you, this city is probably exciting. There's always something happening. It's always the same thing, though. I suppose it's my fault, too. I set the clock with my hands. I rewind the lever on the music box. After a while, you'll notice it, too, ____.

You must be surprised to find this. To be here. I understand. It's very different, isn't it? You'll come to love it, though. At least, that is my hopes for you. I will meet with you soon, but I thought, to be polite, I ought to write a brief introduction to you prior, alongside some rules and a word of advice. I am Edward. I am the founder of Nowhere. **The city cannot thrive without me.** It would simply vanish, shrivel away and die. Because of me, this city continues with its many kinds of inhabitants. I don't want to spoil the fun of exploration for you, but I will say, be very careful not to anger any of them. They're more *fun* at an observable distance.

Now, before I conclude, you must know that there is no way out of this city. I'm sure you took note of it, but the train that brings residents in melts away once they arrive at the station. There is simply no train out, and the city itself has no gateway. Now, read closely because this is important. Should you choose to leave and attempt to leave, I will have the Faceless Few teach you to do otherwise. **You simply cannot leave.** Also, you do not want to make an enemy out of me. Although, I have great faith in you. Once you live here for a few weeks, you'll come to enjoy your stay. I created this city for you, after all. You will enjoy it. **You will not want to leave**.

I will be visiting you shortly. Meanwhile, enjoy the basket of roasted rats that I've sent with this letter. It is a popular snack around here.

Your best friend,

Edwards

The Beige Wallpaper

I heard rooms are built for you
the moment you are born.
I now stay at my new place
in Room 17; fourth floor.

Every room reflects
the mind and soul of its guests.
My wallpaper is an ugly beige,
rusty gold at its best.

I stare at it often
and wonder what it's like,
if I were to tear it apart
and see the other side.

It started as a hobby.
I tore an inch or two.
I stopped for fear of being caught,
but there was something new.

Electrifying excitement,
one I can't explain.
Every tear that I complete,
I feel a blissful pain.

Then I made a discovery,
a mystery wrapped in beige.
Underneath the surface,
there was dripping wet paint.

A tear drop of burgundy
slid down the tear I made.
It stopped a foot underneath
and left a scarlet stain.

Yet I admired its beauty,
I could not tear my eyes away.
That bold red rooted me,
and I coveted more the next day.

Being outside drove me insane,
I felt an itch; a million bites.
If I'm outside my room I think,
I cannot wait for the night.

For when the sun falls,
and the moon takes its place,
I'll be up against my wallpaper,
tearing it page by page.

The more I shred its horrid design,
the more paint falls like tears.
Its crying on the other side,
I can hear it! I can hear!

Oh—it's crying my name! Oh dear,
I feel an itch that can't be pleased.
Unless I have my hands against the wall
tearing recklessly.

It hurts but it's exciting.
Happy pain and happy thoughts.
I tore and tore and tore until
there was nothing else on top.

I realized then as I sat there
with my crimes put to an end,
this wallpaper that I tore
was my very own beige skin.

Edward

It was ninth when I arrived,
five when we met.

I heard the crisp creaks of
my classic red oak board

groaning under the weight of
something

at the foot of my
mellow yellow bed.

Parchment white face,
barely visible, barely alive.

There was no body, nothing to
hold itself upright on the floor.

Ink black irregular ellipses.
So strange I felt the stare.

I felt the contact of
eyes that were missing.

Harbor gray lines,
the hollowed absence,

absence, absence of lips.
A cracked monstrous smile

the size of a crescent moon
up to his very cheekbones.

Wrinkles or cracks or valleys,
his skin fell apart to flesh.

That was Edward,
a floating face.

He opened his mouth to speak.

Edward Likes Coffee

Edward likes coffee,
it's no coffee you've ever seen.
It's what Nowherians call
"rounded-red beans."

The first time he showed me,
I was really scared.
I didn't fully trust him,
but he seems to really care.

He said to brew the beans
you plant them first like
fallow fields on your skin.

Let them grow,
then harvest them,
then do it all again.

So I stayed up that night
a knife in my left
uncertain and afraid.

For Edward?
Was it worth it?

Must I really be this brave?

He's the only one I knew here
and he might know the way out.
I closed my eyes and clenched my teeth
to prevent me from a shout.

With one quick blow
I set in stone
a valley with its seeds.

The beans formed
collected more,
and it began to sting.

I dropped it in his mug.
He drank it with a smile.
"Good job ____,
that's the best I've had a while.

I will come back for more,
so be a dear and keep planting.
Your bittersweet rounded-
red beans taste enchanting."

I was a farmer in the nighttime,
a barista in the day.
No espresso, cappuccino,
only Edward's way,

I had to keep searching
for land to grow the beans.
I began to run out of
spaces in between

the scars.

A Man With No Organs

I met a man with no organs
sipping latte at the café.
He motioned me to sit with him
and asked about my day.

His belly's carved wide opened,
hollowed out for all to see.
You can see his coffee fall from
his throat onto his jeans.

He told me in a solemn voice,
"Beware the formless man.
Under his curse, of which is worst,
I've been cheated in his plans.

Before his eyes, I gave my life.
Yes, gave myself away.
I didn't think my givings would
lead me to my grave.

I gave my heart to a woman,
who ate it and then left.
My kidneys for a nice ol' car,
which I lost to unlucky theft.

My stomach for my addiction
for coffee and them pills.
My liver I traded out for
a fairly unfair deal.

Miss I hope you learn from me
don't trade yourself away.
I gave it all to gain it all
but got nothing I'm afraid.

I wanted to be more than just
another on the streets.
I wanted so badly to become
the best that I can be.

But look me now I'm empty,
I'm hollow like a cave.
I bet the Face is waiting
to dig me up a grave.

I have no organs in me
I have nothing left to lose
won't chat with you no longer
for I'm jumping from the roof."

I Met Depression

I threw on my sweater
in the ninety-degree heat.
I don't know why I'm so afraid
of what others might think.

But serving Edward became
my first priority.
It agitated me when
I wasn't making coffee.

I rounded the corner
to find a withered bed,
underneath a skeleton
with an old woman's head.

She had tufts of wheat hair
and eyeballs bright and big,
cheekbones deeply carved,
and curved, chapped lips.

I was going to move on,
until she called me, though
barely moved her lips.

"Come here young lady.
I promise I'll make it quick.

I want you to know
how I ended up here.
Some word of advice
and things you should fear.

Edward isn't
who you think he is.
He's running up a show
to keep you in a bliss.

I mutilated my wrist
just to serve him tea.
And now look,
now look at poor me.

He told me kindly
to stay in this place.
Leaving the mattress
is a dangerous game.

He told me I'd get hurt,
so I stayed here all alone.
But then my legs gave in,

and I had to call this home.

When my flesh became food,
Edward said he didn't need me.
I opened my eyes to see
who he was and can be.

Heed my warning.
My dear, you're still young.
His name is the Face,
whom you should run from.

Now go! Go on!
Don't stay here too long!
The longer you stay the more
Nowhere becomes strong!

He'll keep you here,
run along dear!
Remember me
and those whom you care.

See the longer you stay,
people disappear.
The memories of those,
those whom you care.

So hurry now

go.

The Face

I think he knows now,
but I can't find a train.
I don't want to serve more coffee,
so please go away.

He's persistent, I find
him every corner I round.
A weathered, wicked smile,
and no body to the ground.

"I've heard some rumors,
words running around.
They say you're trying to leave
to find a way out."

The Face laughed.
What disgusting cackle.
"There's no way out,
no ride you can tackle!

Fine! If you should
be so ungrateful
to my kindness
and very unfaithful.

Fine! If you should
disregard my name,
but now you've entered
my dangerous game.

Fine! If you should
refuse me more things.
I am the king and
more powerful than you think.

Fine! If you should
refuse my friendship.
I offered my 'hands,'
but you wanted away with.

Fine! Because miss,
you'll come to love it.
My city; *your* city,
you can't do away with

I will hunt you down.
I will never leave.
Welcome to nightmares,
farewell to dreams.

I am the Face.
I brand my residents.

Welcome to Nowhere,
where I am the president.

Fine! If I should have
no coffee to drink.
You will find, ____,
you fit in more than you think!"

I Met Defeat

It wasn't till weeks later
did I meet defeat,
curled in the alleyway
and staring at me.

"He's right you know,"
Defeat croaked.
His whimper was sad,
so I halted my stroll.

"Who?" I asked
and stared at his legs,
like a pen on concrete
melting away.

"The Face, he's right,"
Defeat gave a sigh.
"He said we will stay here
until our time to die.

No use running
or hoping for a way.
Make him some coffee,
a better use of your day.

Day; one day to a month
a month to years,
it'll be quick
you'll find you're still here."

Remorse

It was midnight,
a midnight ride.
the cabs are dead,
but the busses still alive.

My fault for being early,
a long time to wait.
If only this night
the bus wasn't so late.

For a car screamed by,
and I caught a glimpse
of a tall-legged monster
with a permanent grin.

Baring teeth with dripping blood,
and the same with his sockets.
I fumbled for my phone
inside of my pockets,

increasingly aware that
the street was now quiet.
No human in sight,
no one to help fight it.

As always I'm left
to my own defenses,
with grim understanding
that I am defenseless.

I happened a blink,
and in a blink of an eye,
he loomed in front of me
a terror in the sky.

I took flight pass streetlights,
my empty cries for help,
like a frog being choked
its helpless croaks and yelps.

And after awhile
the monster was gone.
The chase has ended,
but I could be wrong.

The bus arrived,
and I hopped right in,
glad to be home
safe walls and within.

But safety is a reverie,

comfort is a lie.
When the lights began to flicker,
I knew I was to die.

I watched his shadows emerge
from under the door,
collecting together
from the ceiling to the floor.

Before he fully formed,
I ran in my closet,
praying to God
that I finally lost it.

But in the silence
I heard his roar:
"Come out, come out!
I'll count to four!"

One is an inhale.
Two is a heartbeat.
Three is my remorse,
on four he will find me.

Through the cracks,
I see his face.
Through the cracks,
so ends the chase.

My Memories

I adore these cobblestones
that reflect the lights
beaming from their heads.

The streetlamps engulf
their vessel through their mouths
and leave them hanging dead.

How ravishing a sight to see,
a line of hanging remains!

How delightful, like Christmas lights,
are their eyes that glow away!

Beams from the streetlights
in those dead sockets
fill the limps with spirited life.

Light the road,
the gum and stones,
like stars under the sky.

No, I can't help but grin
with grim intentions

at the dead that hang like banners.

They deserve it.
They all deserve it,
for their sinful words and manners.

He Buried His Dog

I met a young boy today
who buried his dog in trash.
I couldn't believe what I saw,
I asked, and then he said:

"My dog is dead, enough is said,
I see no reason to explain.
His body's now just a lump of flesh
I simply feel no pain.

For we all live, but are we alive
if death awaits at the end?
No miss, for I argue that we are
dead and will die again.

So tell me miss, why be upset
I dump him in the streets?
He's just an empty vessel
a mechanical work without a beat.

My dog here's just like you and me,
we're creatures with no soul.
We might as well bury ourselves
in trash to die alone."

Learning How to Write in Nonfiction

Learning how to write in nonfiction is a bit like going to therapy for the first time. You realize there is a lot more trauma than you had initially understood going in. Today, my counselor told me about the "little t" and the "big T." Little trauma. Big trauma. My big T is being sexually assaulted. My big T is frequently sitting on a broken bridge praying to God that a gust of wind would push me off because I didn't have the strength to do it myself. My big T is shattering a picture frame because all the knives were hidden in the house, and I couldn't stand it anymore, so I took a shard and left fifty scars all over my legs. My big T is hiding underneath my table at night because I think the Face is out to get me, and I was going to die. My big T is cussing out God using His own scripture for a whole night until my parents could calm me down. My little t is like how I told my friends in a long essay about how I was depressed, and all they could say was that they would pray for me. I doubt they did. My little t is like how I was on four different medications daily and how they were constantly switched because the only outcome of the pills were shaky hands, nausea, exhaustion, and a blurred vision. My little t is waking up to my alarm, feeling an empty weight, a meaningless existence burrowing into my brain, and skipping school, telling myself, "Tomorrow is another day." Learning how to write in nonfiction is bit like learning you're more fucked up than you realize, and you tell yourself "I need Jesus, I need Jesus" but you don't go to Jesus, you go to knives and desks and bridges and the comfort of your bed. Learning how to write in nonfiction is a bit like realizing that the City of Nowhere isn't an imagination but a messed-up reality.

The Staircase to Nowhere

How do you expect me to save myself
when the stairs lead only down?
How do you expect one to climb upwards
if in this world you are one-way bound?

A door leads to another,
another to a door.
Before I knew, it can't be true,
I'm a million meters above the floor.

I'm descending a staircase to Nowhere,
to Nowhere I will go.
Every step I take the path behind
dissipates into an airy flow.

I've tripped a thousand times,
rolled down these stone-cold steps.
My legs are tired and weak and sore,
and I can't perceive the building's depth

For I continued to walk for miles,
a million steps I've overcame,
but this staircase that leads me nowhere
continues with no aim.

I feel defeated in my strength,
for I ask myself this and more:
What is the meaning of life, to keep walking,
if I'll never find the end or the door?

What is the point in trying,
when trying is a fool?
Wise is the one who's given up,
who's thrown away their youth.

For nothing comes of working hard,
no fruit is produced by hand.
This staircase that leads me Nowhere
has reminded me that I can't.

I can't do this, I can't do that.
Going Somewhere is a fool's dream.
It seems I have found myself stuck
in the City of Nowhere's scheme.

The Deafening Ring of a Million Notes

At the bottom of the stairway
was a rusty, red theatre.
Frozen in time; holding its breath—

still.

Suffocating, cool air,
suffocating,
with the taste of iron, death, and rot.

Drawn garnet-colored curtains.
Drawn, as though to protect the room's secrets.
Drawn—I am curious.

I sit down on a broken sponge of currant color.
A single note cues the waves of heavy fabric.
The gate opens to reveal

nothing,
but a single note.

That's a simple note of "a,"
I thought
as though the lost part of me was familiar to

this single string of a note.

Following like disciples,
an assembly of strings bow.
A piano in the center.

The sound was soothing,
ripples in a puddle,
but puddle to a lake before a raging sea
with wind so frantic and sailboats engulfed.

I feel so small.

Raging seas scarcely ends within two measures.
This crescendo carries on,
the notes a cacophonic whirlwind.

It's becoming too loud.
I shrink in my chair.
There's a deafening ring of a million notes.

It encloses me,
condemns me.

I feel so small.

Clangoring of chaotic notes—
pots and pans
and glass shattering,
a blossoming argument
unfolding in my ears
DIE! DIE! DIE!
A madman on stage!
An furious dissonance!

If only it would stop!
If only the curtains would draw!

It only gets worse,
Louder and louder—
DIE! DIE! DIE! WHY WON'T YOU DIE?
a deafening ring of a million notes.

It stops.

In the center of the invisible orchestra
stands a man I'm all too familiar with—

the Face, conductor of
a deafening ring of a million notes.

Blackout

My poor, poor index is
fandango from the futile flicking
of a mounted switch that
mocks me like the metronome
sitting in dust on my piano—
click clack click clack.
It sees no end—the night sees no
                end,
and I see, I see
nothing
unless you count the abnormal
figures and shapes,
some hardly recognizable:
the table conjoining with the
floor with the wall with the clock,
becoming a one and a whole
and a reluctant monster, who,
just birthed, has no real
skeleton to keep him from
melting apart in the moonlight.
—And you would expect 1AM
to be a still snow piece,
but Nowherians lose control
over what they do not know

(—and oh, do *we* not know).
The terrible union of *us*, our
cluttered clangoring of stools
giving in to our weight, and
picture frames committing suicide
off the nightstand precipice,
among the shadows that disappear into one another,
oh—the clashing crash caused by a
clown, who with two big feet
and no eyes, leave destruction
in her pathway of
knocked-over trash cans and
gatherings of spilled pills,
the clown being me and
me in the kitchen swimming
to find a match.

Well—
he's wrestling with her next door in the dark,
I'm wrestling with myself in the dark.

And my neighbor is snoring
(poor man doesn't even know what happened!)
but my mind is a timid squirrel.
I look out and

oh,

  why the view ought to change someone,
  ought to make me believe in something or
  someone—some—some God with that
  brilliant moon over a dying, obsidian city.

The Single Sharp Shard I couldn't Throw Away

My art teacher told me to never use black or white,
Not on a palette with the blue, yellow, red.
It ruins the colors, ruins the colors.

If I wanted some shadow, I couldn't use black,
not black behind the two-dimensional shapes,
but blue or purple or something achromatic.

If I wanted some light, I couldn't use white,
not white outlining what should be a sphere,
but yellow or orange or a mix of the two.

I think black or white should be locked up.
Where? I don't know where, maybe
in the chambers under my marble-made pillow.

Maybe behind the creaking floorboards of 11 or
the clock that marked when my parents got home
or in the drawers—yes, the drawers.

Underneath the trash of miniature bells and bags
and yarn, buttons, and receipts I would not throw,
in the red box, I locked that

black or white.

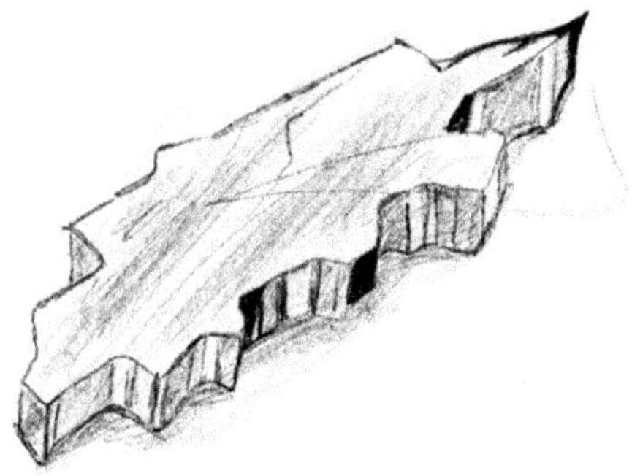

Studying a Knife for Too Long in X Parts

I

When I first held it,
it was wintry and dense

and it tugged on my
yellow, tanned twigs.

I was to cut the can of
aiyu jelly into an unerring

country fallow field,
each movement to leave

a deep, dark gash.
It was soft, and the knife

exhaled into the surface
with such ease and eloquence

that I never thought it would
be my own arm

seven years later.

II

I always knew I would
become an artist.

Colors came as naturally
as holding a knife.

With my first paint brush,
I published my first story,

a tale of blue and red.
The figure skating bristle

became an X-acto knife,
and the frostine white paper

became a timid yellow canvas
with thin, pink paint.

III

If I study a knife too long,
it becomes the apartment.

The sleepers and the parties
are painfully unaware

of when the sky holds her breath
save for the occasional zephyr.

The somnolent apartment
dips himself in the ink

and leaves an imprint
on the pliable pond.

The impression makes
the sconces look like lanterns

dozing off on the surface,
and bobbing to a beat

I cannot hear.

IV

When we dissected a rat,
we learned about

the various organs,
and I think about how

if I was dissected
I would probably have none.

V

A metallic shark fin.
A steel, sharp fang.

Disorderly.
Inviting.

VI

I remember the first time
I studied a knife for too long.

My brother was in college,
and we went to visit him.

They left me alone to
a half-eaten birthday cake

and a knife daubed in
carmine red icing.

And I thought the cake
could be me, and

the icing could be me,
and I held the knife

as a freshman thinking
it was a familiar sentiment.

VII

The knife was a crabgrass
that I pried from the backyard.

I took him by the tuft of his hair
and revealed his spider legs.

He had overstayed his visit,
and by the time I put him

in the trash bag, his friends
had already turned my yard into

scribbled graphite I was
too tired to erase.

VIII

The wind has no business
becoming a knife,

biting the outlines
of my blemishes.

IX

A knife is a pepperoni pizza
that your empty stomach

covets on a late summer night.
One cut of pizza will never

be enough for you, so you take
two cuts of pizza. Then three.

Soon, there are no more pizza,
no more skin on your body

for a cut.

X

I studied a knife
for so long

it became an
unlit cigarette

that I can't smoke
outside.

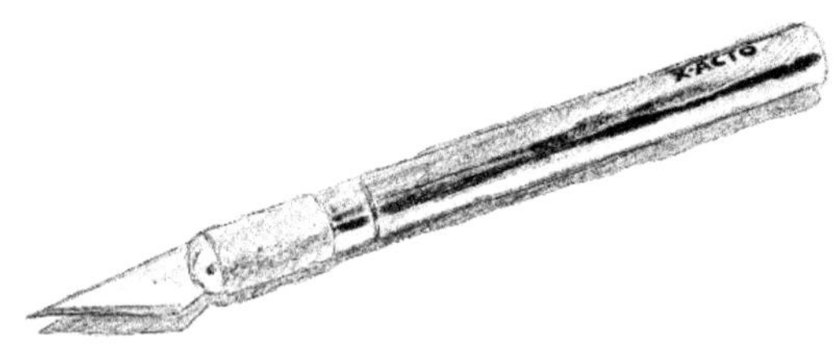

Tore the Page

People and places,
names and faces,
have no strings attached.

Summer burns
with every turn.
I breathe and light my match.

Can't hurt me now,
those vile frowns,
I've set it all ablaze.

This crayon's down
to a stubby brown,
I've gone and tore the page.

Scribble that face,
scribble that place,
scribble where I'm scared.

Don't mess with me,
I've learned to be
a paper in the air.

Off with your head,
and in your stead,
sea cerulean blue.

But angry marks
are leaving scars
outside of my brain too.

Don't ask me what happened.
I can't remember a thing.
I smile day by day.

I broke my crayons.
I pressed too hard,
pressed too hard and tore the page.

An Unusual Plant

Weed.
Resilient to pry apart the man-made grey,
and they sprout; thorned and spider-legs,
and intertwining; phthalo green, jagged cloud
with shriveled slices of sun-kissed apples.
How else can I describe
these ears that poke out from
the photophobic building and into
the coin-colored light of the City?
Ears that fight; overlapping to get a
taste of what the people
have to offer today,
and thirsting, violently, the
delicacy of a
pedestrian's saliva.

Side of the Road

Sometimes I would stand at the side of the road. I would count the cars. How many red ones have passed me. How many blue ones. Sometimes I would stand at the side of the road and count the cars until they become a blur of numbers. A rush of colors, like an artist slicing a canvas with a paintbrush of colors that aren't completely mixed. The Face would hold my hand and give me a sideways glance. He would give my hand a tug. It is a small tug at first. When I refuse to acknowledge him, the Face would float off the sidewalk and pull me forward, hard. When I refuse to move, he would move to the middle of the road, and the cars would screech right through him as though he were a ghost. I know he has no arms, no legs, no body, but I would still feel his hand, some hand, gripping mine ever more tightly, pulling me, tugging me. He calls me by my name. Not the name my mother gave me when I was born. Not the nickname everyone calls me because Chinese is too difficult to pronounce. It is a hollow name. "____," but I know it is mine. It is mine and only mine. He would tell me it is okay, that it won't hurt. He would tell me to trust him. He knows I want to. I would take a step forward. Then, I would hear my name from Elsewhere, and the

Face would disappear and suddenly the cars would become more than just blurs of colors. They are people too.

Bubble Gum and Ash

You breathed me in,
you tapped me out,
I'm free-falling from the sky.

Have no control,
I dance like leaves,
gentle winds as my ride.

Found the ground, and I flicker
for just a spare moment,
but die under his feet.

I am just ash
and used like that,
a little speck in defeat.

And what do I expect from you
to peel me from under
those dirty school tables?

To put me in your mouth
like I haven't been chewed
and left without my label?

What a teasing idea
to think you wouldn't care
that I'm uglified and gross!

That I'm chewed up,
and I'm used up.
No, you'd throw me by the road!

Leave me alone,
I'm used and old.
I'm bubble gum and ash.

You ask me why,
but you know I'd try
to rewrite my shameful past.

I Tried Some, Too

There are new pills in this city,
pills of cobalt blue.
They're wonderful, most brilliant—
I know, I tried some, too.

Everybody takes them now,
there really is no shame.
Everybody needs them now
to overcome their pain.

Step right on up! Go get some pills!
We're running out of stock.
The city is now barren except
the drugstore down the block.

You'll take one first, then you'll want more,
it's two then three then four.
You take them till you've overdosed
and passed out on the floor.

They're fighting in the streets for pills,
it's chaos in this place.
I joined them and burned down our homes,
our sins we can't repay.

For what are we to do when morning comes,
sunlight on our scars?
Heavy head and feeling dread,
our hands forever marred?

Course the answer is so obvious,
for when the morning comes,
our anguish of being alive
leads us back to where we're from.

Here am I in line again,
I await another dose.
Rinse and repeat; I get my treat,
my demon and his host.

The Faceless Few

The untenable crimes
and the muffled shuffles
of the Faceless Few.

To have an identity
you'd be an anomaly.
All the pernicious things they do.

Close your doors and windows,
shut your curtains and your lights.

Here comes the Faceless Few
with pasted faces that are shy.

They cannot speak or smell or see,
these are the Faceless Few.

The precipice of oblivion,
waiting for their cue.

I wonder if I'll be like them someday,
my fate I can't undue.

To be so lost and lowly,
to be the Faceless Few.

Discord in My Veins

We cannot fool ourselves.
The dust collects in the corners of our room,
and when the moon highlights me,
I'll be in the middle of disharmony and rue.
I'll have my arms raised
in mild distaste
of the discord that ensues.

It's a natural plight,
any cloying hope is a fraud.
Any accismus to the roaring night
would render a sarcastic applause.
To welcome it,
a sea of rejects,
the discordant ballad.

In dizziness and frantic laughs
you won't find me the same.
The Faceless Few they trace me at
the outlines of my pain.
To be at the core
of this crazed bore
and have discord in my veins.

I Met a Victim in Nowhere

Two-legged; split.
Blood gushes from this walking clothespin,
leaving a trail as if to make a statement.

But she's a strong girl.
He shoved it between her thighs, then ripped it out.
In and out; over and over like
a greyscale seesaw
till she tore from thigh up,
perfectly symmetrical,
a canyon to her head.
He stopped at her head and left her crawling on two
just so she would be breathing through
an unending beat.

And she told me,
bloodshot eyes she told me,
"I will find them," she said,
"I will find them," she said,
"and when I do," she said,

"they're going to want to sew me back together."

The Day My Friends Died

Isn't it strange how the words "I'll pray for you" can make you feel two completely different ways? When my mother told me "I'll pray for you" with her glassy carob eyes and a deep hue of eminence under them from the many nights she wept for me, I saw, for a flickering second, the single sconce that still worked beside my front door. Whenever my friends said, "I'll pray for you," what it really meant was: "I won't pray for you, but now that I've said that, I've done what it means to be a friend and you cannot hate me for it." What it really meant was: "You're weak. You have to be. Otherwise, why are you depressed? Why do you want to die, and why do you cut yourself?" What it really meant was: "Now that I know all this, she's out of the competition. I'll be the one to give the speech at graduation." And what I saw was my friends shredding each other behind their backs over grades and tests and essays so much so that they didn't realize that they died. Their mangled corpses always said hi to me in the hallways but never stopped to hear beyond that. I couldn't care enough to carve their coarse names onto the crooked stones, and I left no flowers.

Wet Hands

Who cut off his hands
lain in the center of insipid eyes
that he must bear the burden
of spewing water rhythmically
for the stillness of the woods?
Who
has ever stopped and looked up
to gaze at caged cries and think
thank you for all you've done
and what you are?
Who took the chisel
and toiled the seasons
without a bed to lay his head
—and yet!
Who
turns away from the serried sculptures
as though to say
you're never enough.

Dry Bones

There is an unwanted visitor
between your pewter grey thighs.
He hacks the door open every
day and welcomes himself.
You've mastered the art of
dry bones. Dry bones—
looking to the right and
avoiding sordid eyes more
ebony than the cavities that
sully his harbor-hued heart.
Dry bones—those hollow
kisses, hollow affirmations,
a car with no passengers
accelerating to a precipice.
Dry bones—you never wear
lipstick, you don't want
to leave a spoiled stain
on his cheek for him to leave with.
He's taken enough of you
already. Dry bones—he knows
you are on four different daily
medications, so you're too
depressed to fight back, you are
a Spanish fighting bull who,
however abused, never responds to

the matador and the muleta.
Dry bones—your brother is just
down the hall. You could call him,
but what is the point in that?
You've practiced dry bones for
so long you could vividly taste
the orange wind of West Texas
carving your ribcage, sculpting
a piece that will be discarded
to the dogs or the dirt.
Dry bones. Dry bones. Dry bones.
Dry boner between dry bones.
In the beginning, you tried to be Ezekiel.
You prophesied as commanded,
you raised your voice—live! live! live!
—but the rattling never came,
the tendons, the flesh, the skin,
they never came, the breath of God
never came, and it never will.

Paper-Thin

If it was up to me,
then I'd take a layer off.
I'd fold my paper-thin skin
into a paper-thin plane.

It'd take off and get lost
in infinite rain and flickering chartreuse.
It'd disappear into a better place
where I don't belong.

Or somewhere my paper-thin hopes
would tremble in the turbulence,
crumple up and fall flat on cobblestone
with a lonely, paper-thin *plop*.

Rear-View Mirror

Cannot peel my eyes away
from the picture to the right.
He's on my rear-view mirror
stealing all my sight.

That ghastly white face,
wrinkles of many years,
and I began to question
when did he get here?

He has sockets for eyes,
but I know he is staring,
through my skull, into my soul
and all the things I'm wearing.

And a caved-in smile,
wickedly entertained.
Dry and chapped, bloodied and cracked,
feeding from my pain.

No, I cannot look ahead
when the Face is right behind.

Refracting my past like it's such a laugh
in this hideous stormy night.

With every streetlight
it just gets clearer.
I'll wreck my car if I keep
staring at my rear-view mirror.

Out of My Skin

I wonder what it's like to be under their skin,
to live a different life and walk around just fine
without restless breathing and breathing within?

To crawl out of my skin and be someone new.
To crawl out of my skin and not be me.
To crawl out of my skin and be anyone else.
To metamorphosize and to be free.

What I'd give to be in their flesh!
What I'd give to not be me!
What I'd give to throw my skin away!
To shed myself and bleed!

Oh to be perfect; oh to be kind.
Oh to be loved; oh to be wise.
Oh to be wonderful; to be so insouciant.
To be out of my skin, for even a moment.

Meaningless

I didn't know what it meant at first,
not the *pitter patter*
a country away,
not the twitching tufts
that fade in cloud's arrival.

How could I,
another spade behind the bench,
written in the fangs of sparkling towers,
know
why ants travel miles of scorching land only to
become what
          he traverses?

Ring

When he
slapped
me with
both his
hands my
ears rang
sharp
like the
sound of
the ambulance
tearing
through
the hushed
night sky
to take
me to
the hospital
trying to
bleed
myself
dry.

Bloated Figures

Bloated figures down the river
I'll never be the same.
Bloated figures in the waters,
some things will never change.

They say if you throw someone
into the river streams,
as they're devoured by the fish,
you can wish upon a dream.

So day and night they're throwing
some people over banks.
They whisper their heart's desires,
some things just never change.

The smell is foul from miles away,
the people here agree.
Yet the same people keep wishing
and adding to the stream.

A man grabbed me once by my neck
and had me join the rest.
I flailed my arms around the water
right above my chest.

"Pleasure and power
it isn't too much.
It's all I want.
I don't ask for a bunch.

To the gods!
The river stream!
Whoever listens,
here is my dream.

Here is the girl
to satisfy hunger.
Pleasure and power!
lightning and thunder!"

So now I am left here to die
with people of the same fate.
Those bloated faces, bloated legs
I stare in such distaste.

They're skeletons with skins
of discolored mysteries.
Holes of which their soul must've left
and tragic histories.

The ones that are still breathing
grab me and they groan:
"Oh help us stranger, help us please,
kindly take us home!"

They crowd me, and they drown me,
I cannot breathe at all.
They're pulling me in murky waters,
I hear their muted squalls.

Bloated figures that were used.
Tonight I meet my end.
In my dying vision
I see Edward, my old friend.

Empty Desk

The reason why
the desk beside
you is always
empty is because
your classmate
wakes up in
the morning to
her alarm and
feels a warm
pain choke her
throbbing heart
until she can't
breathe, so she
turns off the alarm
and closes her eyes
and prays for sleep
and tells herself
tomorrow, we'll
try again tomorrow.

I Met Stress

A rusty nail—two rusty nails
extended like my forehead
dug on opposing sides of his
          disfigured shoulders,
and a spider's web loops an unending
circle, hugging with no boundaries
the burning skin of metal,
leading to a pile of
          debris.
Umber brown, round, and squared
lumps of burdens with only a
thread and bloody nails.
          Cursed man!
To toil and drag under the
merciless sun, and upsetting glares.
The uneven concrete tugs
his injured shoulders all the more
          Cursed man!
In this City of Nowhere
to leave a trail of a crushed cans and crumpled bags
of chips.

Tower of Bodies

I met a bodylayer.
I asked him what he does.
He's building an infinite tower
in the center just because.

He wants to reach the heavens,
oh to feel the clouds.
He better keep on building,
gotta make his momma proud.

He drives a dump-truck to the river
to load the corpses there.
He picks the parts that he likes best
then drives back to town square.

"Just watch and learn from the best,
I'll show you how it's done.
To bodylayer is an art
and can be tons of fun.

I like torsos as the base.
They're big, sturdy, and broad.
Another limb or torso is
one extra step towards god.

Get your trowel and mortar,
spread it on his chest.
Now gently put a leg on top.
Good! I'm quite impressed!

Visit me from time to time,
within months you will see.
I'll be higher than you all.
Witness my ascendency!"

Just like he said some months ago
the tower grew and grew.
Soon we couldn't see the top.
It disappeared into the blue.

Then one morning I woke up
a rumble through my walls.
The tower started trembling,
the bodies began to fall.

It all collapsed and left the square
a landfill of the dead.
The only thing they found of
the bodylayer was his head.

The City of Nowhere II

If people aren't crazy ,
and I'm not insane,
then why does the rain keep
leaving red stains?

An avalanche from skyscrapers,
a knife between her breasts.
The garbage can is set on fire,
a girl missing half her head.

The boy sewed his arms together,
we have thorns in our veins.
My neighbor just lost both his eyes,
and my friend just lost her brain.

The trees are upside down here,
if there is any at all.
The streetlights flicker because
they're tired of lighting up our flaws

The bridge is cracked and caved in,
bubble gum line weeds and cracks.
The bricks have blood pouring out of them,
a whip mark on his back.

The scrawny can't walk any longer,
they fall and become dust.
The ivy leaves have ears on them,
and there's a rapist on that bus.

Graffiti on the wall that says
you can't ever escape.
People fall like it's a sport
on every typical day.

The swimming pool reeks of rotten flesh
and so does the river downtown.
Beware the woman with scissors,
she will cut open your frown.

This is the City of Nowhere,
I can't find a way to leave.
This is the City of Nowhere,
where I will always be.

The Grand Buffet

There's a grand opening downtown
of a new buffet,
which specializes in all kinds of
dishes and different plates.

It costs some fingers to get in,
I got some from the park.
There are so many people
inside this work of art.

Murals of angelic scenes
with pillars of ivy spades,
and rows upon rows of tasty goods,
I begin to stuff my face.

Lasagna, beef, my favorite things.
There's hibachi in here, too.
The hoggers how they push and shove,
fighting for a way to get through.

Time has passed, I cannot stop,
the people 'round me too.
Before we knew, our buttons popped,
our bellies grew and grew.

I headed to the restroom
to find a trail of blood
leading to some double doors,
I entered with a shrug.

Inside I threw up instantly.
Customers hung from hooks.
Their bodies bloody, broken, beat,
frozen with a look.

I heard a knife against a board
only yards away.
I peered across some bodies,
wishing I never stayed.

The butcher and the cook have been
feeding us ourselves.
Our greed and our gluttony
had put us in a spell.

I ran outside and threw up
for nothing more is true
humans are disgusting
and this much is not new.

It's Raining Upside Down

Rewind my whole life,
I'll pay any price
to make everything undone.

Every single mistake,
red drop in its place,
collected into one.

Dirty water seeps,
from red dirt it creeps,
blood over the ground.

I'll raise my arms
and feel the warmth.
It's raining upside down.

It's raining upside down in Nowhere,
the blood's flowing to the sky,
crawling from my toes to my chest,
to my cheeks and past my eyes.

It's raining upside down in Nowhere,
I orchestrated this.
Lightning connects to my hand
in an energy of bliss.

It's raining upside down in Nowhere,
and it won't ever end.
Let it flood the skies to a sunset life,
take me back to where it began.

Rewind the tapes,
they walk backwards.

Unmask yourselves,
a crowd of actors.

My cuts are sealed,
my skin is white.

The suture is slithering
out of sight.

Watch my glory
as I take it all back.

Watch my glory
fade from black.

Bring your umbrella,
but there's nothing to fear.
Darling it's raining
upside down in Nowhere.

Meaningless II

Who do we think we are?
Translating the creation of unseen lips,
formless giving birth to form, and yet,
we have the audacity to transpose
the kind wars of almon-shaped leaves
or the entrancing highway of ravines
lumping and diverting on an ancient being's hand,
or how sometimes we just *know*
of true love and molecular bonds and ghosts,
as though raising the key would render our creation
our imitation, duplication, recreation
to be better than the beauty of the wrinkled earth,
to be better than a bud, or even resembling a bud.
Why do we do the things we do?
Arched backs, slouched, not a penny to bear,
suffocated under the weight of a ceiling,
and the ghost of art that haunts us

found me stubborn full of
springtime bubbling bloom and wildflower sun
now cursed to chase a moon that with unseen limbs
run a mile when I only a foot,
outstretched towards something, perhaps nothing,
but a reflection of what is truly great.

Who do we think we are
except a gashed corner
possessed to work a wheel
that no one will even glance at.

"Kill Myself"

is a universal joke that I don't find funny. My friends do though. It is their favorite joke. It is their best joke. They will say:

"Yo _____, what's up?"

"Studying for a chem test lol. I have an essay to write for next period and then I gotta study for UIL."

"Oh my gosh same."

"Yeah, *kill myself.*"

And they would all laugh and say:

"Bro saaaame." "You're such a mood." "Honestly thoughhh." "It be like that sometimes."

It's so comical, the art of wanting to die. The art of crossing the road without looking both ways in hopes that the driver is too busy on their phone to notice you. The art of situating the tip of a bitter, biting blade against your wrist and hoping courage would strike in another minute, another hour, another day. The art of staring down a balcony and rewatching your own body splatter the concrete ground. It is comical. A really funny bit. It's so amusing that, every time someone says that, I imagine them taking a kitchen knife and tracing it from the top of their head down in five equal sections. I imagine their face, their hair, and every part of their skin falling apart, opening, blossoming, like an almond flower, revealing a head composed of raven scribbles, eyes you cannot see, and though they become demons like everyone in the City of Nowhere, they will never be a resident.

I Didn't Want to Be Brought to This World

Children who didn't ask to be born.
Children who were brought to this world.
Children who wished they were dead,
the ugliest children that I've ever met.

Children with tear-stained eyes.
Children who cry day and night.
Children whose fate is sealed,
to invisible hands of an unfair deal.

Children who are now all grown.
Children who are dead and old.
Children who didn't ask to be born,
I didn't want to be brought to this world.

A Distant Blue

Somewhere, why are you so far?
If I climbed up my apartment complex,
if I stood on my toes,
if I pressed myself against the railings,
even on the rooftops,
you are a distant blue.

Somewhere, do you exist?
When I raise my head,
when I affix my eyes to what is ahead,
when I gather the courage to believe,
you are only a distant blue.

Somewhere, will you wait for me?
Wait for me wherever you are?
If I try harder to see,
you become a distant grey.

Somewhere, do you hear me?
Or are there too many colors in between?
Should I paint it all blue so that we may be closer?
Should I color myself blue?
And if I should, would your colors change?
Somewhere, where'd you go?

Everywhere I look
in all four directions
the east, west, north, and south
you are a faint memory—

a distant blue.

4AM

To be bound in the four corners of a reverie,
four minatory faces; same blank looks.
Four obstreperous, repeating melodies,
all the same; a floor all too familiar
and a ceiling that is overweight.
Dark room with nothing but my window's light
that highlights and derides the curves of my shame.
Four are the shadows sneaking around.

A thick miasma of anguish; it covers my frame.
Another hour, and I'll have overcome the night,
but the Face is crafty in his ways.

A fantastical nightmare of your unseen laminate.
You persistently observe me from
the land of the revenants.
I am not insane! I know this much is evident!
But four is your face, and four was my medicine.

Her Dress

I started from black ink
black; bigger than a blotch
reflecting man-made colors and fly-covered
oranges,
and I continued,
smooth and no longer afraid
of death and
wherever the white lines want to take me
with four wheels
and a ukulele underneath
the wind pricks me teasingly and reminds
me
that I'm alone.
They intruded my dreams,
those selfish figures,
crossing the streets without a care,
with complete trust of my morality
and inebriated red lips of laughter and
liquor—

I want her dress.

I want that world of not
knowing,

drunk towards the air I'm breathing and
uncaring to my black car.

I ended in a line, a narrow line of a little speck
like a fly outside your window
looking in
only a dot, and
my journey comes to a stop
with the turning gesture of my hand.

I Made Friends With a Corpse Today

I made friends with a corpse today,
we met at a local diner.
He said he liked my ears,
said nothing looked finer.

I made friends with a corpse today,
he told me how he died:
took too many pills, fell off the wheel,
and spread his wings to fly.

"Look, you can tell I fell from high
just by how my neck appears,"
he twisted his crooked neck
till his skin began to tear.

"Don't be like me, took too many pills
cared for what they think.
Give me your ears, no need to hear,
they'll lead you to the brink.

I know you hear them voices
telling you that you can change.
Your ears, they lie! Trust the dead guy!
Our deal we can arrange.

Give me your ears, and then you'll know
the peace of silent nights.
Trust in me, for I'm your friend,
your friend would never lie."

I thanked him for his kindness,
then gave my ears away.
I cannot hear, but I can see
his face begin to change.

As blood poured down the sides of my head
I see this corpse is not my friend.
As he transformed, I realized he was
the Face playing pretend.

Hey ____,

How are you? You missed school today, and yesterday, and the day before. You've...actually been gone for a while. Truth is, I'm very worried for you. You know I'm here for you, right? I've been writing letters for you a lot, but I don't know if they reach you. If they do, please, if you can, write me back. We're all really worried for you.

Today, ____ and I went to McDonalds together after school. I know you know this because we invited you. We walked together, while you opted to just drive car alone, but you never showed up. I was really worried. A few hours later, ____ told me you tried to drown yourself. Why? Your mom didn't even know about it when we showed up at the door with ______ too. She had no idea what was going on. We were all very worried. You shouldn't drown yourself, ____. You're a good friend of mine. Think of all the jokes we've made together. Remember when we first started talking? We really got to know each other in that dual-credit class. That professor was so mean! It was really fun with you in it though. We always had each other to complain with. Oh, remember all the times we went to Skillets together?

Our little dates? It'd be a shame, too, if we couldn't get a caramel frappé at McDonalds after school together anymore. I hope you haven't tried to drown yourself again. Remember our friend Ryan? I can't lose another friend. Also, who else am I supposed to send memes to on Discord? Ugh.

Please, just reach out if you can, okay?

Forever your girlfriend,
your go-to K-pop recommender,
your personal meme-dealer,
your source of spontaneous energy,

What are you doing dork?

Haha, are you ignoring me?

I know, I know it's 3AM.

Hello?

...

Are you okay?

Oh. Why are you crying?

Hey, it's okay, you can talk to me.

Oh. It's okay if you don't want to talk.

[click]

...

[ding]

[ding ding]

[ding ding ding ding]

[________ Instagram: Here's some cute pig memes. Cheer up you dork, ok?]

Behind My Church

If the barren concrete of crazed yellow lines
should hold its breath and remain silent,
then I'll whisper here my final prayers.

And if the pointed green that upholds the cross
should stare at me with no recognition,
then I'll lock my car and leave.

Further and further
that winding path
of mud and weed
and tractor tracks,

of wildflowers,
whose name unknown,
and the tallest grass
harass those who dare roam.

A familiar path
to a familiar place,
behind the church
that's far from grace.

The path becomes

serried trees,
shrubs and other
pointy things.

The wind tickles them
abusively,
and I happen to catch
a crumpled leaf.

It's used and chewed,
wearily escaping.
It fell off the tree
after months of waiting.

Sentimental
when I realized,
I'm just like this leaf
that fell from the sky.

Past the trees,
here's my destination:
the broken bridge
of my desperation.

I walk the narrow beam,
my feelings numb in my skin,

unafraid of the forces,
not the waves nor the wind.

This is it,
the end of the road,
end of the bridge,
my new and true home.

No going back,
I left my prayers
underneath me
pointy wet layers.

The water will catch me,
and so will the stones.
This is it ,
the end of the road.

Hold your breath,
lean into death,
I will count to three.

Behind the church,
the weed, the dirt,
there you will not find me.

A Twisted Body

I woke up in a hallway,
a corridor red and bright
with old fashioned designs like some hotel
abandoned; but still alive.

I don't know how I got here,
nor do I know why.
I was a little tired
and began to rub my eyes.

When my vision cleared, I saw
a twisted body at the end.
He stood and watched me with a smile,
his body a sinister bend.

His neck a twisted 360,
his arms a mangled mess.
His stomach looked like a rope,
his legs like a bird's nest.

A twisted man with a twisted body,
he smiled a twisted smile.
At the end of this corridor,
he stared for quite awhile.

I froze up and didn't know what to do.
He's staring right at me.
Next thing I know, he's running
at me at twisted speeds.

Then I woke up.

A City Underwater

It is raining today
against the thick see-through skull,
waging war against the squalid city
            and wouldn't you know

            know; no, I don't
not the who, the why, the where,
not the when, the how, and
perhaps that is why I'm not there.
Perhaps that is why I'm not the ghost
dodging crystal bullets
or the shadow slug and
his hole-infested umbrella.

I am not there, that is why I'm not there.
Soon the murky waters will reach
the borderland between parietal and occipital,
and I'll have to come to terms with my state

            I am not okay.
Someone miles away is playing around with a switch.
The on and off like the hands of a broken clock
cursed to snap up and down with a click of the
tongue.

Someone miles away is flicking the switch.
The room lights up, and then it's black again,
and then a second of an earthquake.

Soon the whole city will be engulfed
with its streets, wrinkles, and people,
and they will be forgotten.
It's already happening.

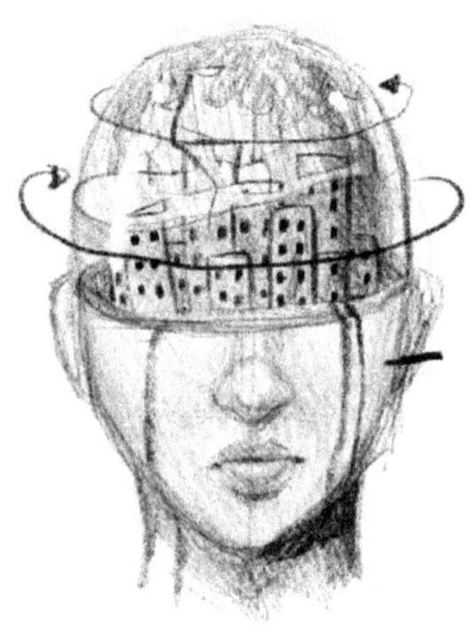

I Like My Shadow More Than My Flesh

Flat and no figure
flimsy, fleeting of fear,
two-dimensional
and free of care.

Fluid on the concrete,
like water on rocks,
carving those edges
a smooth, paved flock.

When it's time to hide
the shadow shies,

joins the others
her sisters and brothers.

Your footsteps don't hurt her,
she is what she's on.
Her lack of character
is what makes her so strong.

A marionette to me,
but she has it better.
Voice unheard, but
never under the weather.

It's nothing I can hide
or can't attest,
I like my shadow
more than my flesh.

One-Way Ticket to Nowhere

The courage of some people
to impersonate my experiences,
to disregard them completely
by throwing a scene.

"Poor, poor me.
Oh—poor, poor me.
Me and my perfect life,
oh poor me. Poor me."

They gather rings of chrysanthemums
and whisper words of prayer.
To what god? What god
will listen to you?

I know you, and you, and you.
You and your troubles
find refuge in a place I can't even see,
frolicking in the sunflower fields
of Somewhere.

To what reward is your public lament?
You pick off a poor rose's soul and
toss them left of you between sniffles

your only medallion is eyes and mine
of disgust. Stop pretending.

You don't belong in this place.
You belong way over there.
Prove to me and show me
your one-way ticket to Nowhere.

Tired

I'm so tired of existing,
each day is much the same:
same people, streets, same song, same beat,
someone please take me away.

I want to leave, I want to escape
this City of Nowhere.
I asked around in desperation,
but no train leads to Elsewhere.

The truth is I belong here
in this miserable grave.
The truth is that I fit right in
to these different darkened rays.

We're all lost souls, so we're at home,
yet I still wish to leave.
Won't someone take me away
to a better place at least?

I dream of nights about a time
before my train ride here,
of happy times and foolish rides,
and of someone I hold dear.

What is his name? I oft forget.
I wonder where he is.
Elsewhere, perhaps?
Somewhere better than this?

Does he remember me when I forget?
Does he even know my name?
Is he out there, maybe Somewhere,
on his way to save the day?

Carry me away from here,
take me on your wings.
Carry me with your arms of love
away from everything.

I fantasize too much I think.
I belong here after all.
I'll stay inside this city.
I will die within these walls.

Hello?

Dummy?

Haha, hey dork, what's up?

Hello?

I can't hear you.

Hold on, I'm at tennis. We just finished.

What's wrong?

Hello?

I'm scared.

Where are you?

I'm on the side of the road...I wanted to crash.

Hey, you're going to be okay dork.

...

You're cutting out.

...

Hello?

[click]

Learning to Freeze

My therapist told me that there's three different reactions when the human body senses danger: fight, flight, or freeze. Fighting has a noble connotation attached to it. When you watch movies or read books, it is often the fighters that are crowned heroes as they should, having done something that requires immense amounts of courage. Flight doesn't have quite as much of a noble connotation, but, out of the three, it is usually the most logical. Running, though cowardly, is a smart thing. I've heard of fight or flight, but I had never heard of freeze until that therapy session. Freeze is the side character you hate the most in a horror movie. Freeze is the character that gets eaten, murdered, and killed. Freeze is not noble and very irrational. Freeze is, well, me.

...

I always saw demons growing up. Perhaps, as my mother once phrased it before, it is the curse of an artist to have a vivid imagination. When I finally moved out of my parent's room and I puffed up my chest to brave my own bedroom for the night, I remember distinctly how much effort it took to fall asleep. We put my bed in the corner so that I may press my back and my head and my trembling shoulders against the walls, so that I may view the whole room in its entirety. No demons to sneak up behind me. No demons to creep by on the side. Still, I saw the shadows lurking, swimming across the floorboard or smirking in the midnight smoke behind my closet doors. I knew they were there. I made them. I gave them names. And all their faces I recognized. My blanket was my barrier, my shield and fortress, and so was Jesus. My alarm clock had a radio system attached, so I would put on KSBJ and lower the volume so that I could just barely hear the words "So let go my soul and trust in Him, the waves and wind still know His name."

...

One time I stood in the middle of the road and froze. A single scarecrow stalking the street. There were no cars though.

...

I started to see the Face more and more often. He talks to me frequently, so frequently his voice would blend into mine and become familiar. Sometimes, I welcomed him. His company wasn't all that bad. Sometimes, he scared me. Sometimes I hide under my table. *He wants to hurt me*, I think to myself. *He's going to hurt me. I'm going to die. I'm going to die. I'm going to die. I'm going to die.* And it is true. I am not crazy. My hand holds a knife but never for defense. I think, *This is it. This is it.* I think of my writings, my poems. They raid my mind, they raid my mind like intrusive people asking, "Are you okay? Are you okay? Are you okay?" I think, *This is it. This is it. This is it. The water will catch me, and so will the stones. This is it, the end of the road. This is it. The end of the road. This is it. The end of the road. End. End of the road. The end.*

...

One time at school when they were having a pep rally, I saw the lights flicker all around us. Demons. I heard the Face, his laugh, the way it bounced off the hallway lockers to reach me, to possess me. He was loud. He was louder than me. *DIE. DIE. DIE. WHY WON'T YOU JUST DIE. JUST DIE. DIE. DIE.* And I had to cover my ears and run to the bathroom stall. I locked the door and nestled myself in the corner, just as I did as a child. I froze. I learned that it was no battle I could win. I learned that there was no point in fighting, and you can't outrun him. I learned to hide. To freeze. Even still, I knew he was there. The lights were out, and the Face breathed against the door. *Come out, ____. Come out. Come out. COME OUT. LET'S DIE. LET'S GO*

AND DIE. COME OUT. COME OUT. DIE. DIE. DIE. DIE—

"____?" ... "____, are you okay?"

"No."

"Where are you?"

"The last one."

And _____ got on her knees and peered under the stall. The lights were on. She laughed. "What are you doing?"

"It's loud."

"Yeah." _____ squeezed herself under the stall door and risked smearing whatever germs infested the high school bathroom floor onto her clean clothes. "It is loud, isn't it? I hate pep rallies too." She sat across from me. "We saw you leave. ____ and I are really worried for you."

"..."

"The hall monitor said we need to get you out. I guess they think you're doing drugs or something haha."

"That's so stupid."

"Right? Forget drugs. The most we'd do is drink too much frappés and crash from all the sugar."

"Frappés sound really good right now."

"Right? When was the last time we got ourselves some?"

"It might've been just a few days ago."

"Oh right. Haha." ... "Hey, you want to get some after school?"

"Yeah. I'd love that."

"Come on. Let's get you out the restroom first. This place is naaaastyyy. Plus, you don't want to stay on the floor. God knows what's been on there."

And I think, for a moment, that maybe, just maybe, I can see a glimpse of Somewhere.

Rehema

I used to be the ancient architect who,
from the ground of their consciousness,
erected the cathedrals of the playground.
I made ghosts out of guitars
and hosted missions, tumbling across
the cold, wooden floorboards with
keen cat eyes and a heart of adrenaline.
I used to jump behind barricades
and lead my army to victory with
my cunning calls and hollowed noodles.
They drowned and we had bruises,
but that was okay.

I used to princess my own palace until
they barged in and pried my legs apart.
We dug under roots and made homes for those
lonely acorns that couldn't be bothered to move.
We named them names long gone.
I used to be a popstar, rockstar, the wild wings of a
golden pink microphone on top of a bed frame
with no bed. Me and my fairy friends
fended off our foes.
Our wings broke occasionally,
but that was okay.

We didn't care, we didn't care.
We still don't care,
but for the wrong things.

My cathedrals collapsed under the weight of
your dump truck's generosity.
I realized they're just plastic with bolts anyways.
My guitars were out of tune,
and the enemy caught me mid-roll
(I think my partner gave me away).
The pool's empty now, go home.
My tiara is battered,
and my plastic high heels' outgrown and missing.
They cut the tree down, and
I can't remember the acorn's names.
My stage is just an empty frame,
and our wings were cut off.

Seesaws, swings, and slides substituted for the
sound and smell of smoke and slurs.

Porcelain Hands

I had a dream last night,
a good one, for once.
You were there, dummy.

You held my hands,
and I felt the cold touch.
I opened a freezer and graced my fingers
on the walls.

You, your hands.
You were never warm,
though perhaps before, perhaps before
in the kiln, they burned your
kaolin clay hands.
It hurts to think of it, but
see how far you've come.

They're precious works.
I have yet to thank the ceramicist
for your porcelain hands.

You are a wall away, one
flat, chipped black mirror away.
I don't know where you are,

but I think that is fine.

You'll be at the station
when I arrive.
You will be at the station.

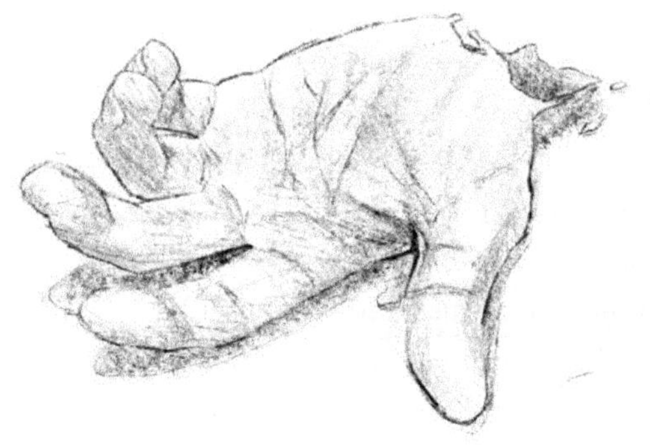

The City of Nowhere III

This is the City of Nowhere,
my home for almost four years.
This is the City of Nowhere,
where no one ever cares.

This is the City of Nowhere,
nothing much has changed,
except every new resident,
this city's much the same.

Like raining dead and red coffee,
blue pills, buffets of flesh,
waters of fat fish and limbs,
and a town square that's a mess.

After years of living here,
I'm starting to believe
that this place of self-loathing
is the only thing life has to bring.

Like this City of Nowhere
is the only place on Earth.
Like there is no Elsewhere,
I question my unfair birth.

I've checked the station at Northwest,
I see that he is right.
There is no real way out for
the train melts when it arrives.

The train only comes from outside.
I'll stay here till I age.
No Elsewhere, Somewhere; Nowhere is
the home for which I'll stay.

It's pretty tonight.

Yeah, it really is. It's cold too.

Yeah, sorry. I'm sure you want to go inside.

I just want to spend the last moment with you here.

It's okay dork.

...

Are you crying?

No, I'm not. You are though.

Nuh-uh. Your nose is all red.

Your nose is all red.

You know where I really want to go with you?

Huh?

I want to go see the Northern Lights with you.

I'd love that. We can bring all our animals too.

Our future shiba, corgi, cat, pig, lizard, turtle, bear, hamster, bunny—

—giraffe, fox, owl, bear—

I already said bear, dummy!

Okay, well, two bears. We'll bring all of them!

Mhm! And and and then we'll be in the snow!

We'll make snow angels—

Snow ball fight! We'll have a warm cabin—

With s'mores! And hot chocolate!

Hot chocolate with marshmallows!

And then the colors baby! The colors of the sky!

I can't wait to see it all with you.

Me too dork.

Can we make a promise?

Yeah!

We'll always be together. No matter what.

No matter what!

Promise?

Promise!

Paper White Thighs and Naked Nights

It was mesmerizing like crickets,
in some kind of harmony,
though, sporadic and unorganized the same.

That was his voice,
so common and unheard like lips in the ocean,
at least to my ears and my senses.
Something in me desired something
beyond a static screen and a thick pane of glass,
beyond that choir,
cicadas and ocean waves and
the crunch of dead leaves.

I didn't feel any understanding there,
except the understanding
that a labyrinth stays a labyrinth,
as I, the turtle, stay a turtle,
forever cursed to round a corner,
the same corner,
and be a villain.

The Faceless Few remind me of the word
meaningless. Meaningless, what is
meaningless?

I can't upset myself from believing with utmost certainty

what meaningless meant

it meant I was never meant to be.

So I opened my door
inside my paper white thighs and naked nights,
and the Face embraced my inner spine,
rejoicing in our reunion,
and I surrendered all I thought I was,
and every ounce that held on.
I let go to find nothing else
but a cold, crooked crown
calling my name as my finger
danced nervously but almost with
anticipation, and I realized it
was five, it is five, you have to
go before the sun can rise, it is
five, they will wake so go and take
that knife you have and—

In Between Worlds

Brushstrokes in the Air

How blue is the blue?
Why very blue indeed,
like neon lights and summer skies,
like clear seas and the ocean breeze.

How green is the green?
Why very green I say to me,
like pastures with herds of sheep,
like fields of flowers for the free.

How yellow is that yellow?
Why very yellow my good sir!
So yellow like the morning sun
or the dandelions that stir!

How white is the white?
Oh so very white my dear!
Like the first snowfall of winter
or cotton fields of every year!

How orange is the orange?
Very orange I guarantee!
Like orange of the fruits in trees,
like the reflection in the sea!

How pink is that pink?
Yes, that pink of that very sky!
Like pink carnations or peonies,
like the pink clouds of a sunrise!

How purple is the purple?
Why the purple is a lot!
Like the bruise of hands from punching walls,
like the bruises of my thoughts.

How red are those brushstrokes?
How red is the paint you use?
How red is that wrist you slit?
How red is your abuse?

How red is your floorboard?
How red now are your feet?
How red is the knife you dropped
you dumb-sick-fuck, you freak?

How magnificent is the sky!
How could one ever create
such delightful work of art
for us to appreciate?

It’s cold down here, but that’s alright,
the lights above still dance.
I wish to go up there some day,
I wish to see something so grand.

I wish I could live longer.
I wish I wasn’t a fool.
I wish I’d live another day,
a year or so will do.

For in eternal sleep there is no
beauty of this kind.
Beauty to be shared by those
I love and consider mine.

This masterpiece is fading,
yes, it’s flickering away.
Those colors that I’d love to see
only one will remain.

It’s red I see and nothing else,
what shameful deed I’ve done.
I could’ve went up there, up north
to see the lights above.

He holds my hand in that safe place
where colors dance and gleam.
Brushstrokes in the air; I see us
holding hands in unity.

Lift your head girl
won't die just yet.

The Music of the Sirens

At the end of the hallway,
the sound of a music box
plays endlessly.

ping ping ping

With every little step,
it grows clearer
and calls me by my name.

The music of the sirens.

ping ping ping

We hear it all the time,
but we choose to ignore
its grim tale.

ping ping ping

I'm here at the end,
a rosewood box that
glows red and blue.

The music of the sirens

they're here.

[hush]

Blue and Red

on the trees.
Blue and red on the leaves.
Blue and red in my hair.
Blue and red everywhere.

Blue and red tiles.
Blue and red for miles.
My blue and red door.
Blue and red on the concrete floor.

Blue and red across the street.
Blue and red against my feet.
Blue and red fighting streetlights.
Blue and red on this sad night.

Blue and red on my hands.
Blue and red sweeps like a fan.
Blue and red on tree barks and grass.
Blue and red are really fast.

Blue and red paints my garage.
Blue and red a rude barrage.
Blue and red might save my life,
blue and red might let me die.

If blue and red don't get here soon,
if blue and red show up forenoon,
then blue and red will glow upon
my dying corpse bathed in the sun.

Elsewhere

Elsewhere

You're alright. It's going to be okay. It's going to be okay. Where are you hurt?

Alright, hey hey hey. It's okay. We'll get you inside the ambulance to check it out, okay? You don't have to worry about it.

Just follow me.

____ what's going on?

Are you her parents?

Come on, follow me, right this way.

Be careful, the steps are kind of high. There you go.

I'm sorry.

Don't apologize.

He's going to examine your wound okay?

Do you have anything to bite?

Uhhhh…do we?

No.

That's fine.

We're going to unwrap it. Just keep your eyes on me, okay? Talk to me. What happened?

I slit my wrist.

You slit your wrist?

Yes.

With what?

An X-Acto knife.

Why?

I wanted to die.

Did something happen?

Uhm.

Sorry.

It's okay.

Here. Why don't we do this? Tell me about your day. What did you do today?

Uhm. I woke up. I had breakfast.

Where?

McDonalds.

What'd you get?

A sausage egg McMuffin.

What else did you do?

Uhm. I don't know. Teenager stuff.

Like what?

I studied.

That's teenager stuff?

Haha. I don't know. I watched a movie with my boyfriend.

You're boyfriend? *Ooh*, what's his name?

______.

So a movie huh? At the theatre?

No. I screen-shared.

That's teenager stuff?

I guess.

________, what did we do as teenagers? Man, I don't even know. That was decades ago. But studying is not teenager stuff.
You have a lot expectations? Academic-wise?

Yeah.

Your parents?

No, just from me.

Well, you know when I was a kid—

Tch—

—I didn't study at all. I didn't even know what I wanted to be haha.
There you go. It looks like you stopped the bleeding yourself. Good job. You're lucky. Would've had to apply a gauze and that stuff hurts like a bitch.
Can you feel your hand at all? You wrapped it really tight. Your hand is purple.

No.

Can you feel this?

Not really.

Alright. I've loosened the wrap more, so hopefully your hand will feel better. It's really deep though. We're going to have to take you to the hospital to get some stitches. Does it hurt?

I can't feel anything.

Alright. ________ here is going to go and talk to your parents and the others about the situation real quick. Are you fine with riding with us to the hospital to get your stitches done?

Yeah.

Alright. Keep talking to me. Do you have a history of hurting yourself?

Yeah. I have a lot. Here. My arms and legs.
It's kind of hard to tell in this area though.

What's your medical history?

I'm sorry?

Do you have a history of depression?

Yes.

Tell me more.

Depression. Anxiety. Dissociation.
Bipolar. Suicidal thoughts.

So what were you thinking about before you hurt yourself? Did something cause it?

No.

Anything bad happened that day?

Kind of. Not really.

What do you mean?

It's really just me.

…

I'm scared. I guess. I'm scared I won't live up to expectations. I'd rather die than make another mistake.

How about now? Who called 911?

I did.

So you don't want to die, right?

No. I don't.

What changed your mind?

Uhm. I want to go there.

Where?

To the north.

What's up north?

The Northern Lights.

Oh yeah? It's a beauty.

It is. I wanted to see it with him.
I promised to.

Elsewhere II

Mm mm mm, so you're ____?

Yes sir.

Ah, and are you aware of how close you were? *Too* close. Way too close. D'you know that? Way too close.
Here, this will hurt a bit.

Yes ma'am.

Way too close.

Tch—

I'll be back.
Yes ma'am.
Way too close. *Tch tch tch*. You know that? Way too close.

Tch—

You need to listen to sum classical music. Thas' right. Classical music. Thas' way too close.

Classical music?

Yeah yeah. Mozart shit. You know? When you're feeling like this? Thas way too close.

I'm more of a Beethoven girl. Or Chopin.

Beethoven! Beethoven's good! I play his songs. Yeah yeah. He good.

What do you play?

Why I learned piano couple months ago. Bought one of them old and used ones from some old, broken-down store. Cost a lot, but the piano still sound good. My wife complain lots though. I play too much. *Haha.*

Oh really? I play piano, too. It's just the same.
But that's how you learn a piece.
You gotta play it over and over again
to learn it. So my family has to listen
to the same thing over and over.

Oh you play piano too? Why piano—why I love piano! Girl. You way too close though. How you gon' play if you slit you wrist? Tell you wuh—you like Beethoven righ'?

I love Beethoven.

You listen to them classical pieces when you sad like that. Or play piano. Thas way too close. You cut your wrist like dis' how you gon' play piano now? Way too close girl. Way too close. You know that? You listen to them classical pieces or play piano. They make you happy. Feel a certain way.

A certain way?

You listen to them classical pieces you ain't wanna die. No no. Beethoven was deaf, deaf as hell, and this dude still played piano. He ain't killing himself. No no. But you way too close. You know if

Beethoven can be livin' an' playing them pieces all
deaf and shit, you cans too. Sure as hell can.
All done. You listen to them classical pieces, alright?
Don't be doing nothing stupid.

Somewhere

Jehovah Shammah

Maybe in the shadows scattered on this
worthless, rich dirt
will I find the one who says "I Am."
Maybe for all that it is worth,
His presence colors the sand,
and if I shuffle my feet up this land,
will I find Him in the angry cracks of tree barks?
Tree barks like the veins in His hands?
If I stare at a cloudless sky, will I find Him?

I find the truth to be unbelieving.
I never felt you, but I never tried.
I cursed like branches in the storm
blinded by anger and lies.

But I find you in the unexpected,
the blurs I once ignored,
now receptive to your presence
I find you at the core.

Your invisible body lays,
the earth, the skies, the seas,
awaken to my senses
you have helped me to believe.

You are the cotton that covers me,
you are the sand, seeds, and stone,
you are the cicadas' melodies,
you are the necklace that I hold.

You are the table that shields me
from the blanket of darkness outside.
You are the morning dew that gently
calms my naked thighs.

You are the bathroom stalls
that cover up my shame.
You are the bathroom tiles
that collect my tears of pain.

You are my blanket cover
in the middle of the night.
In restlessness you find me
and tell me I'll be fine.

You are hidden in my scars
a blessing in disguise.
No valleys nor mountains,
no walls you cannot climb.

You were the bandage
that I wrapped so very tight.
You were the strength in me
preventing me to die.

You were my shaking fingers
spelling 9-1-1.
You were the only reason
I had strength in me to run.

You were the rushing ambulance
that sliced the country road.
You were there for my parents
and allowed them to be bold.

Perhaps I have forgotten
Jehovah Shammah.
You have never left my side
to you I stand in awe.

You are my ticket to Somewhere,
you are my train ride there.
With you all around me
present; I won't fear.

All the Doors of This Corridor

And I will let all the doors of this corridor
fly open; break the locks.
Let the doors slam against the wall
like an ancient war drum beating.
Let the doors be opened
and let them all out.

I'm tired of being frozen,
of hiding like
there's nothing I can do.

I don't understand myself,
but I'm tired, I'm tired, I'm so tired
of hiding underneath this table.

No, it can't protect me forever
from the monsters behind the doors.
Let them fly open! Let them be free!
Let me stand in the middle of it all!

Yes! Come at me with all your strength!
All the doors at once!
Come at me with your mighty roars and hisses!
Come at me! Flood this old corridor!

I'll be here at the end!
Come at me all at once!
I'm not afraid.

So let the doors of this corridor fly open,
let the monsters be set free!
I'm tired of these locks.
Come at me all at once!
I'm not afraid.

For Ryan

When I lean against
the balcony and feel
compelled to climb over,
I think about how
Ryan could've been
in college by now,
a star musician,
whatever he pursued,
he would've succeeded.
Don't forget your friend's
grave. The cemetery is
a solemn intersection
with overgrown weed
and vehicles, his coffin
a carnation, a stretcher.
_____ cannot lose another
friend, don't do that to her.

And in Heaven, Ryan
looks down and says:
"It isn't time yet, ____.
It isn't time to come.
You still have much
to do." And every time
I walk away from
the balcony, I feel
a little, proud smile
somewhere between
the outlines of a cloud
and the never-ending
stretch of arctic blue.

Dry Bones Revisited

A moment before I swiped the knife, I closed my eyes and begged—Please! Please! Please!—before I threw open the Bible, and it landed on Joel 2:25, and it said: "I will restore to you the years that the swarming locust has eaten, the hopper, the destroyer, and the cutter, my great army, which I sent among you," and I begged—Please! Please! Please!—but the verse meant nothing to me at the time, so I swiped at my wrist, and when I felt something warm and wet rapidly coat my foot, I turned the light on, and I saw the inside of my wrist, and at first the pulsing flesh was a cool hue of periwinkle purple before a thick wine-colored icing oozed, collected, and fell, and I dropped to my knees and cried and stopped breathing, and I saw the Northern Lights, and I saw my family, and I saw my boyfriend, and I parted my lips and whispered, "Please God," and I was given the strength to find my gauze, to find my wrap, and I tried to start it, but the blood kept coming and the bandage kept slipping, and I said, "Please God, please God," and the bandage finally caught on, and I called 911, and I ran out the door, and I hurried the operator, and I felt my head grow heavy, and I thought I was going to die, but the ambulance took me away, and the doctor said that it was very close to cutting my artery, and something stirred in me when the doctor began to stitch, and it felt like a thump, a tiny ripple, like you know something is about to happen, like the beginning of an avalanche, and my heart throbbed, and I realized the dry bones were rattling because the truth is I never was Ezekiel, and God knew that, and He heard me whisper please, and so God said "Live!" and the bones shook the ground, and the tendons sprouted when the doctor stitched my wrist, and the flesh sprouted when my wrist closed, and the skin sprouted when the doctor removed the lacerations, and all I was left with was an army and my healed scar.

The City of Nowhere IV

This is the City of Nowhere,
it has no hold on me.
Today I have decided
that I will break free.

This is the City of Nowhere,
my dummy by my side.
He came for me to help me escape,
it's time to fight or die.

This City of Nowhere is nothing to me,
it has no strength or power.
It is only a place that I have stayed
because I was such a coward.

Come at me with all your strength,
this City of Nowhere.
Its people come to take me down,
but with him I do not fear.

Overcome the odds; the monsters,
the faces, demons, ghosts.
Overcome the darkness and their traps,
don't forget what matters most.

You're stronger than you think you are
and brighter than you see.
Your soul is like an iron giant
against these empty streets.

They're nothing against you girl,
your strength comes from the soul.
Fight back those who oppressed you
strike back with pain tenfold.

Hold my hand and just believe,
we'll make it there alive.
The exit is right at the end,
across the river, on the other side.

Across the bridge stands my old friend,
my foe who haunts me still.
Edward, the Face, that formless being
a monster created by my will.

You've nothing against my heart,
I made you in my mind.
I created you to haunt myself,
to hurt myself and cry.

Away from me you filthy thing,
you were never my real friend.
You lied to me, disguised to be
a monster in the end.

You're nothing in Nowhere,
you never stood a chance.
You fed on my anxiety,
but now I shall advance.

The Train to Somewhere

I am riding a train to Somewhere,
to Somewhere I will go.
The city of hopes and dreams
where I will thrive until I'm old.

I am riding a train to Somewhere,
for I have Somewhere to be.
My dummy calls my name and holds my hand
he sits right next to me.

I am riding a train to Somewhere,
it leaves a trailing sigh.
The window's vivid streaks of blue
then orange into night.

I am riding a train to Somewhere,
with passengers that come and leave.
Their faces glow like the morning sun
as they're forever free.

I know exactly what it means,
where people go when they leave.
I know why they smile and laugh.
I know exactly what they see.

I will see the painting!
And the mirror underneath!
This train that takes me Somewhere,
takes me Somewhere to be free.

I'll ride this train; I've left my home
I've stayed there for too long.
Soon I'll be where I'm supposed to be.
Nowhere is long gone.

Farewell you wicked fences
that bend now under wind!
Farewell those empty faces!
The downcast and their sins!

I realize that I'm glowing!
Just like everyone else!
We are all on this train to Somewhere
to become a better self.

This train takes no wrong turn right,
I'm headed the right way.
The City of Somewhere, I'm coming.
I will be there one of these days.

I am riding a train to Somewhere,
to Somewhere is where it ends.
Here at the stop, a city,
a place for me to rest.

Dear readers,

Thank you for reading my book. I'm really proud of you for making it to the end. I'm not a poet. I don't pride myself in my writings. I'm a struggling English major who doesn't even know some of the most basic grammar. In fact, I don't even know most poetry terms (or any, if I'm being completely honest). So, really? Thank you for sticking by to the end. It means a lot.

I never learned the foundations of poetry—what poetry is, what makes up poetry, how to write one, etc. In fact, I didn't know I was writing poems when this first came about. I bought a journal during my senior year in high school when, after healing a great deal for a while, I felt my mental health plummet again. I started documenting my thoughts in the moment to make sense of what was going on, and everything I wrote seemed like fragmented, unrelated words. It was how I felt, though. It seemed writing them down in this strange, scattered way was the only medium to express, truly, my situation. It's difficult, and I'm sure a lot of people can agree with that sentiment. There are experiences and emotions that we just can't put to words without some sort of mode. Some things are just meant to be captured in a metaphor, some sort of strange, bizarre image, or maybe a string of what seems to be nonsensical words. Writing became my form of coping.

After my suicidal attempt, I had a long road in front of me to overcome. Poetry became my means to collect my thoughts over the traumatic experience. While I was reading through my journal entries that I had made prior to my suicide attempt, I found one called "The Train to Nowhere." I had written it before to explain what depression felt like to me. I don't know exactly what stirred in me, but I transferred the poem to my computer and wrote a follow-up poem: "The City of Nowhere." One thing led to another, and soon I had seven poems describing my struggles in the form of a strange story. Suddenly, I found purpose. I always believed there was a reason for every little thing, and to me, this was it. I wanted to share my testimony in hopes of reaching out to even just one person and shed some ray of encouragement.

Finally, I only ask to be kind. The world is harsh enough as it is. It might seem small but showing a little kindness and understanding to those around you goes a long way. As for your friends, hold them close. Make sure they know how much they mean to you. And if you don't have any friends, that's okay, too. You'll find one. You can most definitely reach out to me, too, if you'd like.

Again, thank you so much for reading my book. And if you read all of this ending garbo-warbo, thank you, too.

Spread some love and kindness,

Gigi Cheng

Special thanks to

my family for supporting me throughout my journey. Even though mental illness was such a difficult situation to understand, my family still stood beside me and listened to what I had to say. For my mother, Annie, thank you for your words of wisdom, your advice and your love. Thank you for being vulnerable with me at times. For my father, Oscar, thank you for being such a strong foothold for the family. You always stay cheerful and strong in your faith. For my parents both, thank you guys for praying for me, being strong and faithful to God throughout all of this. Special thanks to my wonderful boyfriend, Mario, for being so supportive and understanding. He helped me out of countless episodes and was always so encouraging. Because of him, I wasn't afraid to tackle some of my worst battles. Special thanks to my teachers. Mrs. Crabtree, you always said I'd write a book, and here it is. Mrs. Jones and Mrs. McCrory—thank you guys so much for the love and support. For Mrs. Johnson, thank you for introducing me to poetry, though you might not have known that. Mrs. Rudellat, you were an amazing counselor, and what you've told me still inspires me today. For my professors this semester, I want to thank Andy Wilkinson for being so supportive of my book and my poems. Your class and your advice have made me more open-minded. Special thanks to my church, for the unending prayers and love. Finally, special thanks to my readers, for taking the time to share in this experience with me.

CPSIA information can be obtained
at www.ICGtesting.com
Printed in the USA
BVHW051754060522
636309BV00011B/1206